What Kids Say About Carole Marsh Mysteries . . .

I love the real locations! Reading the book always makes me want to go and visit them all on our next family vacation. My Mom says maybe, but I can't wait!

One day, I want to be a real kid in one of Ms. Marsh's mystery books. I think it would be fun, and I think I am a real character anyway. I filled out the application and sent it in and am keeping my fingers crossed!

History was not my favorite subject till I started reading Carole Marsh Mysteries. Ms. Marsh really brings history to life. Also, she leaves room for the scary and fun.

I think Christina is so smart and brave. She is lucky to be in the mystery books because she gets to go to a lot of places. I always wonder just how much of the book is true and what is made up. Trying to figure that out is fun!

Grant is cool and funny! He makes me laugh a lot!!

I like that there are boys and girls in the story of different ages. Some mysteries I outgrow, but I can always find a favorite character to identify with in these books.

They are scary, but not too scary. They are funny. I learn a lot. There is always food which makes me hungry. I feel like I am there.

What Adults Say About Carole Marsh Mysteries . . .

I think kids love these books because they have such a wealth of detail. I know I learn a lot reading them! It's an engaging way to look at the history of any place or event. I always say I'm only going to read one chapter to the kids, but that never happens—it's always two or three, at least!   —Librarian

Reading the mystery and going on the field trip—Scavenger Hunt in hand—was the most fun our class ever had! It really brought the place and its history to life. They loved the real kids characters and all the humor. I loved seeing them learn that reading is an experience to enjoy!   —4th grade teacher

Carole Marsh is really on to something with these unique mysteries. They are so clever; kids want to read them all. The Teacher's Guides are chock full of activities, recipes, and additional fascinating information. My kids thought I was an expert on the subject—and with this tool, I felt like it!   —3rd grade teacher

My students loved writing their own Real Kids/Real Places mystery book! Ms. Marsh's reproducible guidelines are a real jewel. They learned about copyright and more & ended up with their own book they were so proud of!   —Reading/Writing Teacher

The Mystery on the

MIGHTY MISSISSIPPI

by

Carole Marsh

Cover design: Vicki DeJoy; Editor: Jenny Corsey; Graphic Design: Steve St. Laurent; Layout and footer design: Lynette Rowe; Photography: Michael Boylan.

Also available:
The Mystery on the Mighty Mississippi Teacher's Guide

Gallopade is proud to be a member of these educational organizations and associations:

International Reading Association
National Association for Gifted Children
The National School Supply and Equipment Association
Association for Supervision and Curriculum Development
The National Council for the Social Studies
Museum Store Association
Association of Partners for Public Lands

NSSEA
ASCD

This book is dedicated to everyone who lives, or ever has lived, along the Mighty Mississippi River!

This book is a complete work of fiction. All events are fictionalized, and although the first names of real children are used, their characterization in this book is fiction.

For additional information on Carole Marsh Mysteries, visit: www.carolemarshmysteries.com

Jammin' in New Orleans!

20 YEARS AGO ...

As a mother and an author, one of the fondest periods of my life was when I decided to write mystery books for children. At this time (1979) kids were pretty much glued to the TV, something parents and teachers complained about the way they do about video games today.

I decided to set each mystery in a real place—a place kids could go and visit for themselves after reading the book. And I also used real children as characters. Usually a couple of my own children served as characters, and I had no trouble recruiting kids from the book's location to also be characters.

Also, I wanted all the kids—boys and girls of all ages—to participate in solving the mystery. And, I wanted kids to learn something as they read. Something about the history of the location. And I wanted the stories to be funny.

That formula of real+scary+smart+fun served me well. The kids and I had a great time visiting each site and many of the events in the stories actually came out of our experiences there. (For example, we really did parade in New Orleans, feel a quiver in New Madrid, straddle the start of the river in Lake Itasca, peek in Tom Sawyer's cave, ride a ferry across the flooded river, go up in the Gateway Arch, and much more!)

I love getting letters from teachers and parents who say they read the book with their class or child, then visited the historic site and saw all the places in the mystery for themselves. What's so great about that? What's great is that you and your children have an experience that bonds you together forever. Something you shared. Something you both cared about at the time. Something that crossed all age levels—a good story, a good scare, a good laugh!

20 years later,

Carole Marsh

Christina Yother **Grant Yother** **Sam Ellis** **Jake Ellis**

ABOUT THE CHARACTERS

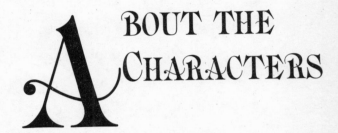

Christina Yother, 9, from Peachtree City, Georgia

Grant Yother, 7, from Peachtree City, Georgia, Christina's brother

Sam Ellis, age 6, as Sam Edwards, age 8; from Peachtree City

Jake Ellis, age 4, as Jake Edwards, age 6; from Peachtree City
(And yes, Luke is their younger brother in real life, too!)

The many places featured in the book actually exist and are worth a visit! Perhaps you could read the book and follow the trail these kids went on during their mysterious adventure!

Titles in the Carole Marsh Mysteries Series

*Books and Teacher's Guides are available at
booksellers, libraries, school supply stores, museums,
and many other locations!*

CONTENTS

Readers, to help you correctly pronounce any words that may be new to you, I have numbered that word or term. Look at the bottom of the page to find the footnote that will tell you how to say the word!

–*Carole Marsh*

1 IN 1814 WE TOOK A LITTLE TRIP

Grant Yother stood in the middle of Jackson Square in the town of New Orleans in Louisiana and sang at the top of his lungs:

"In 1814, we took a little trip
Along with Colonel Jackson
Down the Mighty Mississip!
We took a little bacon and we took a little beans,
And we caught the bloody British in the town of
New Orleans!"

Then his grandfather, Papa, joined in:

"We fired our guns and the British kept
a'comin';
There wasn't nigh as many as there was a

while ago;
We fired once more and they began a'runnin'
On down the Mississippi to the Gulf of Mexico!"

Christina, Grant's older sister, and Mimi, their grandmother, hid their heads beneath the frilly umbrellas they had just bought in the Square.

"I've never seen those two before, have you, Christina?" Mimi asked, as they strolled away from the singers.

Christina giggled and rolled her eyes. "No! I certainly have not. I'm certain that those two are absolutely no relation to us, right Mimi?"

"Right!" Mimi agreed, steering Christina to an outdoor lemonade stand. They ordered two tall, icy lemonades and took them to an ice-cream parlor style table and chairs beneath an ancient oak tree all dressed up in thick beards of long, gray Spanish Moss.

"Isn't New Orleans just the most wonderful town?" Christina said. "I just love all the neat park squares, and the old trees, and the artists at work right out on the sidewalks."

Christina and her grandmother looked around. Sure enough in every direction all types of artists were

scattered around the park "doing their thing."

Nearby a watercolor artist painted a beautiful scene of the park itself. Christina noticed how her palette of colors glistened in the morning sun. Beside her, a photographer had a large camera set up on a tripod and was making a photo of a couple all dressed up fancy, old-timey costumes.

Down the walkway, a mime was acting out a humorous skit for a group of tourists. One of the children in the crowd giggled as the mime magically produced a red rose from behind her left ear!

"Is it always this festive in Jackson Square?" Christina asked Mimi. "It seems like one big party."

Mimi laughed. "Sometimes it does seem like New Orleans is one big party," she agreed. "Especially in the Vieux Carré[1]."

"What's that?" asked Christina. She knew it sounded like French, but she didn't know what the term meant.

"It means French Quarter," Mimi explained. "That's the area all around here where you see the parks, shops, restaurants, museums, tourist attractions, streetcars, and the riverfront."

"Hmm," Christina muttered thoughtfully. She

[1] vu KAH ray

had only been in New Orleans overnight and already she was captivated by the unique city. She and Grant and Mimi and Papa had driven down from their home in Peachtree City, Georgia and just arrived last night.

Mimi was a kids' mystery book writer and had come down here on a trip to research the Mississippi River. Papa was Mimi's official helper, travel agent, baggage carrier, and best restaurant-finder in the world, according to her grandmother. Christina and Grant were lucky that they often got to travel with them, like this time. School had just gotten out. The only deadline they had was to meet their friends Sam and Jake in one week in St. Louis, Missouri for some big Lewis and Clark celebration. Mimi was going to give a speech there.

While it might seem like Christina and Grant just tagged around after their grandmother, the truth was that Mimi had this problem—wherever she went, mystery seemed to follow! She always used her grandkids as real life characters in her books. The locations and the history in the books were always real, too. But supposedly, the story was fiction—made up.

However, as Christina and Grant well knew, it didn't always turn out that way! While Mimi had her

head in a book in some library, and Papa was off checking out historic sites, it often fell to the kids to solve whatever real life mystery came up. That is, if one did—and it almost always did.

But this trip, Christina felt lucky. New Orleans was such a beautiful city. It still felt like spring here with a rainbow of flowers in bloom that smelled so good they made you smile. And the sky was so blue. And the grass lime green. And everyone seemed so happy, like life was a permanent vacation.

Perhaps, Christina thought, this would be one trip that could just be fun. Relaxing. No stress. No strange characters. No weird clues to decipher. No danger. No mystery.

Right?

2 THE VIEUX CARRÉ

Suddenly two big hands grabbed Mimi around her neck from behind. Two smaller hands squeezed Christina's neck. The two girls squealed loudly.

"Surprise!" Grant said, as he and Papa let go of their necks and came around the front of the table and took the other two seats.

"Lemonade! Lemonade!!" the two men shrieked together.

"Singing at the top of your lungs makes you soooooo thirsty," said Grant, adding a few hacking coughs for special effects.

"Acting like an idiot in a public place ought to make you cough," Christina told her brother.

"Aw, we were just having fun," Papa said. "It's such a beautiful morning, isn't it? I have a great day planned for us!"

"What?! What?!" Christina and Grant demanded together.

"First things, first," Papa insisted and rose to get he and Grant a lemonade.

"I can't wait to hear what we are going to do," Christina said. "Papa always plans the best things."

Mimi sipped her lemonade. "Well, I hope he has planned a tight schedule. This is our only day in New Orleans. We need to make the best of it."

Papa had overheard her. "The best of it I have made, indeed!" he said, sitting down and handing Grant his glass of lemonade.

"Then let's hear it," Christina said. She squirmed in her seat; she could hardly wait to get started. They were "burning daylight," as Papa often said. Then Christina relaxed. We have started, she thought to herself. We're here and we're already having fun. Not a mystery in sight. What a relief.

"Okay," Papa said, spreading a map of the French Quarter out on the little table. "First, we're going to the Aquarium of the Americas. That will take all morning, I'm sure. Then we will visit the D-Day Museum that has a lot of World War II exhibits, and then . . ."

"Papa!" Mimi said. "That is more than we can do in four days! Why don't you let Grant and Christina choose? You and I have been to New Orleans lots of times."

"But how do you leave out riding the streetcar, or seeing how they make Tabasco® hot sauce, or riding a boat through the bayou[2] to see the alligators? And then there are all those above-ground cemeteries and vampires! And don't forget the pirates!"

Christina and Grant both let their mouths fall open at the same time. Lemonade dripped down Grant's chin, but he didn't seem to notice. *Alligators? Vampires? Pirates?* What kind of city was this anyway?

Grant and Christina were speechless, but Mimi was not. "These are your grandchildren," she reminded Papa. "Let's pick something nice for kids, like the Louisiana Children's Museum."

Grant jumped up, spilling his lemonade. "No!" he insisted. "Let's pick alligators, and pirates, and vampires. We can go to some sissy kid's museum any old day."

Everyone laughed. "Grant, you'll be the first to get scared at that stuff," Christina teased him.

"Will not!" said Grant.

---

2 BYE YOU; a Cajun word for a backwater creek

"Will too!" argued Christina.

Then everyone got quiet as a mime approached them with a funny look on his face. He was dressed in black tights and ballet slippers. He wore a red and white striped knit shirt with a red rose stuck in the pocket. And he wore a pair of white cotton gloves. His face was covered in white greasepaint.

Christina knew that a mime did not speak. He acted out what he wanted you to know. The mime looked Mimi in the eye. He took the rose out of his pocket and scribbled in the air as if writing in the sky. Then he pointed to Mimi. Mimi smiled and nodded to indicate that yes, she was indeed a writer.

Next the mime crouched down and looked Papa right in the eye. He wiggled his head back and forth as if he were thinking, then he put his white-gloved hand on Papa's heart. Then he pointed towards Mimi. Papa gave a hearty laugh. "Yep!" he said. "I'm crazy about that woman!"

Now the mime squatted down and began to look all around Grant. Then he made a scary face. Next he took his hands and joined them at the wrists. He opened and closed his hands like a big jaw. "Oh, I got it!" Grant said. "Watch out for gators!"

The mime then went into a swashbuckling dance, swinging an invisible sword to and fro in the air. "And the pirates!" Grant added, and the mime nodded.

Christina felt little goosebumps creep up her arms and across the back of her neck. Slowly the mime approached her. He looked very serious. Then he shook as if he were scared to death.

"What? What?" Christina insisted, though she was not sure she wanted to know what the mime was getting at.

The mime waved his hand in front of his face. Then he leaned over so close to Christina's face that she could smell breath mints. Suddenly, he opened his mouth to reveal fangs. The sharp teeth were tipped in red as if dripping blood.

Christina let out a little squeal, and the mime backed off. Then he waved his hand in front of his face again and now had a pair of red wax lips over his lips. He put his fingers to the fake lips and then made a kissing motion and aimed his fingers at Christina.

"The vampire will bite her because she is so sweet?" Grant guessed, and the mime nodded. He took a big bow. Papa slipped him a five-dollar tip for the entertainment, and the mime skipped off with a

wave back to them.

"You didn't seem to enjoy that," Papa said to his granddaughter.

"It was a little creepy," Christina admitted.

"Well, feel up in your hair," Mimi said.

Reluctantly, Christina lifted her hand to her head. She gasped when she brushed over her hair and felt something. She pulled it out of her hair and looked to see the red rose the mime had stuck there. *When had he done that? And how?*

Mimi gave Christina a funny look. "Now," she said, "you're beginning to understand something else about New Orleans."

"What?" asked Christina, confused.

"That it's magical and mysterious," Papa said.

Christina frowned. Only one of those words sounded okay to her.

Grant started waving wildly. He did not say a word, but motioned with all his might, practically turning the table over.

"For heaven's sake, Grant, what is it?" Mimi said.

"You give up?" Grant said happily. "I was miming. I was saying let's GO!"

3 THE CABILDO

As it turned out, that morning they didn't go to any of the places Mimi and Papa had named. Instead, they wandered lazily through the French Quarter, passing shops filled with Mardi Gras[3] costumes.

"I wish we had been here for the big Mardi Gras parades," Grant said. "Think of all the shiny beads and candy they would have thrown down to us from the floats."

"Oh, be glad you weren't here back in February when that annual celebration took place," Papa said. "It is fun, but it's also a real zoo with so many people packing the streets. A day like today is much better."

Mimi didn't look so sure. "But all the Mardi Gras balls would sure be a lot of fun to attend," Mimi said wistfully. Mimi and Papa loved to dance.

"What is Mardi Gras anyway?" Christina asked.

[3] MAR dee GRAH; French for "Fat Tuesday"

She stared into a window at mannequins decked out in elaborate costumes of purple and green and gold. They wore feathery masks decorated with colorful sequins and glitter.

"It's a special celebration held all around Louisiana each year," Mimi explained. "The carnival takes place not only in New Orleans but in small towns all around the state. It's lots of parties and parades. It's been going on for years and years."

History, Christina thought. That's what New Orleans seemed all about. But, hey, she was out of school for the summer and didn't want to think too much about a school subject. But here, history seemed to surround them in the old buildings covered with vines and porches surrounded by lacy black iron balconies. It didn't feel like dead history, it felt like living, breathing history.

"Why does it feel so different here?" Christina asked. She stopped to wipe sweat from her brow.

"That's the humidity," Papa said. "New Orleans is far south enough to have almost a tropical climate. The town is regularly clobbered by hurricanes."

Christina sighed. "Well, it makes me feel drowsy, even though I just got up not long ago." Of

course, they'd had a long drive yesterday, only getting to the Gulf of Mexico around dusk. They had seen a beautiful sunset as they drove across the long bridge over Lake Ponchartrain. It was dark when they got to town, so they had just had a quick dinner and gone right to sleep. Christina had slept in a big bed covered with a lacy canopy.

At the Cabildo[4], a very Spanish-looking fort-like building where the famous Louisiana Purchase had been signed, Mimi scooted off to the library to do some research. Papa talked with the museum's curator. Grant and Christina wandered around the strange building with its dim light and exhibits of Caddo Indians who once lived in Louisiana. Then came the Spanish in their funny-looking metal helmets, and then the French. Most of the history represented seemed to be about war, fighting, fighting, and war.

"No wonder they like to have so much fun in New Orleans today," Christina said. "It seems like their past was pretty bloody."

"Yeah," Grant agreed. "Just look at this picture of all these dead people. The writing says they died in

[4] cah bill DOE; Spanish for fort

a yellow fever epidemic."

"Well, they probably didn't have vaccines against diseases back then," Christina said. "So don't complain next time you get a booster shot."

Grant just wrinkled up his nose and squinted his eyes. He couldn't make that promise.

Soon Mimi and Papa reappeared at the same time with the same thought. "Let's eat lunch!"

As their grandparents hurried them down the street beneath lampposts burning gas flames, even during the daylight, Christina noted, "There sure are a lot of restaurants here."

Mimi and Papa both laughed. "Everyone loves to eat in New Orleans!" they both said.

In a moment they were seated in an open-air restaurant. Their glass-topped table sat next to a fountain that spewed both water and fire at the same time.

"That's a pretty good trick," Grant said.

"More magic," said Christina with a sigh.

"Four Mud Bug Po Boys!" said Papa to the waiter.

"Uh, Papa," said Christina. "I'm not so sure I

want to eat anything called a *mud bug*."

"It's okay," Mimi insisted. "That's just a nickname for crawfish; they're like shrimp—very delicious—you'll love them."

And sure enough, Christina did. So did Grant. And as they chowed down, they asked their grandparents about things they had seen at the Cabildo that had confused them."

"How come people look and talk so funny here?" Christina asked.

"They don't look funny at all," Mimi said. "Many of the people here come from different cultural backgrounds. They may be part French, part Spanish, part Canadian, or many other nationalities. That's one of the wonderful things about Louisiana—it's such a melting pot of many different kinds of people."

"Well, maybe so," said Grant, chewing his mud bug thoroughly. "But they really do talk funny."

Papa laughed. "You probably heard some Cajuns talking."

"Cajuns?" Christina repeated.

"People who came here from Canada long ago and married French folks," Mimi explained. "They often live along the bayous, make wonderful stews like

seafood gumbo, play neat-sounding music called zydeco, and like to dance something called the Cajun two-step."

"We'll show you tonight," Papa said. "We are going to Mulate's!"

Mimi seemed delighted to hear this, but Christina and Grant were busy listening to the music being played by a band that had just tuned up on the sidewalk outside the restaurant.

"Is that zydeco music?" Grant asked. He loved music and dancing, but he had never heard a sound like this before.

Papa closed his eyes and listened to the blowing horns and other lively sounds of the music. "No," he said. "That's JAZZ!"

"Well, where are they going?" Christina asked. "They are lined up like it's a parade, and they have umbrellas, and everyone's dressed up real fancy. Is it a party?"

Mimi gave Christina a funny look. "No," she said. "Actually, it's a funeral. Someone has died. They are headed to the City of the Dead."

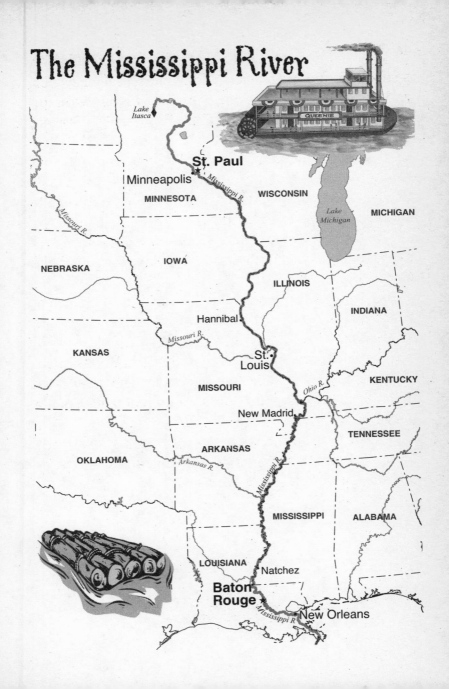

4 DEAD PEOPLE AND ALL THAT JAZZ

"Come on," Papa said, paying the bill quickly. "Let's go see!"

"No thanks!" said Christina.

"Yes thanks!!" said Grant.

"It's okay, Christina," Mimi said. "You really must see how they bury their dead in New Orleans. It will surprise you."

Much against her will, Christina trudged along behind the parade. When the musicians climbed into long, black cars, Papa led them quickly to a streetcar stop. He paid their fare, and they hopped aboard.

"To the cemeteries!" Papa said.

As the streetcar started off down its metal tracks, they lurched to their seats.

"Could we be electrocuted?" Grant asked. He gazed suspiciously at the wires and cables overhead which gave the streetcar its power.

"We're safe," Papa assured him.

Christina stared out the open sides of the streetcar. With a constant *clackety-clack-clack* they sped down the track. Some of the neighborhoods had enormous mansions with tall stone walls hiding them from view. Other neighborhoods were more run down and covered in litter.

After a few miles, Papa pulled a wire overhead which rang a bell and the driver stopped. They hopped off the streetcar and carefully crossed over the tracks. As soon as they did, they entered an eerie neighborhood. It looked very, very old. The large houses were covered with vines and surrounded by walls with big iron gates at the entrance. The houses had tall windows, but all were shuttered or covered with dark, heavy drapes.

The sidewalk was a maze of cracks. Christina and Grant laughed as they tried not to step on any cracks, but it was just impossible. As they looked down at their feet, Mimi called out, "Turn right!" And when the kids looked up, they found themselves in the middle

of the strangest graveyard they had ever seen.

They were surrounded by hundreds and hundreds of small marble buildings, very close to the narrow sidewalk and to one another. They looked ancient. Some of the marble was stained or broken. Christina could see that if you made a wrong turn, you could easily get lost in the maze of structures.

"What are these?" she asked. Then at a distance, she spotted the funeral parade standing near one of the buildings. Their heads were bowed in prayer. "They are tombs, aren't they," she said, answering her own question. "This must be a City of the Dead?"

"Yes," said Mimi.

"But why do they bury their dead above the ground instead of beneath the ground?" asked Grant.

Papa chuckled. "Now Grant, you like science. Figure it out. New Orleans is actually located on land that lies below sea level. And, as you know, the Mississippi River is very close by."

Grant put his chin in his hand like he always did when he was thinking. "Hmm," he said thoughtfully. "So if they buried the dead people below ground...and the river flooded..."

"Which it often does," Papa added.

"Then the dead people would drown?" Grant concluded.

Christina laughed. "Grant! They couldn't drown, they would already be dead."

"But Grant's still right," Papa said. "The bodies would be flooded out of their muddy graves and washed away."

"Probably into my backyard if I lived here," Mimi said with a shudder.

"So they built these stone tombs above the ground to solve the problem?" asked Christina.

"Exactly," said Papa.

Christina stared down the long row of sad, little buildings. Some had stone angels on top of them, or tombstones with cracked writing filled with dirt. A little green lizard climbed over one tombstone. Christina watched him slither into a crack in one of the tombs.

When she looked up, she realized that Mimi, Papa, and Grant must have already headed back to the entrance to the cemetery. Feeling a strange panic in her stomach, she looked in every direction. Through one row of tombs she spotted the funeral paraders closing up their umbrellas, shutting their instruments back in cases, and climbing back into their black cars.

When they drove off, Christina stood dead still.

"Mimi," she said in a tiny voice. "Grrant? Papa?" But there was no answer. There were only four choices of directions to go and Christina could not recall from which direction they had entered the cemetery. Slowly turning around, she gasped when she spotted a black figure disappear between two of the tombs. When she looked down, there was a red rose at her feet. And it had a note attached to it.

"Oh, no," Christina whispered to herself (and any ghosts who were listening?), "mystery's afoot!"

5 ATTACK AT LAKE ITASCA

Sam and Jake Edwards straddled a narrow puddle of water in Lake Itasca, Minnesota. Sam was eight; his little brother Jake was six. They were small for their ages, and so they had to really streeeeeetch their legs to keep their feet out of the water. One stood in front of the other, and they giggled as they tried to keep steady and not fall headfirst into the Mississippi River.

"It's hard to believe that this little bit of water is where the river starts," Sam said.

"Dad said this is the beginning of the river, but Mom said it is way over in Montana," Jake said. "I'm confused."

"That's because it's the biggest, longest river in America," Sam said. "All I know is that its end, or mouth, is in New Orleans."

"Hey, that's where Grant and Christina are!" said Jake. The boys could hear their parents calling in the distance, but they were having too much fun to pay attention.

"Yeah, we're supposed to meet them soon in St. Louis," Sam said. He tottered briefly and water flooded into his left shoe.

"Where's that?" asked Jake. He tottered too, and water swooshed into his right shoe. The water was icy cold!

"Missouri," said Sam. "We gotta get there in a couple of days I think. Christina e-mailed me on Dad's Palm Pilot last night. She said, and I quote, 'A mystery's afoot!'"

Jake shook his head. "No mystery here. Both our feet are wet, and Mom's gonna get us." Suddenly the boys realized that their parents were calling for them again. They looked up and went running for the car.

When they got there, their Mom shushed them. "The baby is asleep!" she warned. "Be quiet and get in the back."

"We've gotta get a move on," Dad said. "Times a-wastin', boys!"

Having fun at Lake Itasca!

Sam giggled. "Dad, you're starting to sound like Tom Sawyer and Huckleberry Finn."

Dad got in the car and started the engine. Their baby brother, Luke, snored away. "Well, why not?" their father said. "We're headed to Hannibal, Missouri— where those fictional boys had a lot of fun."

"Fictional?" said Sam, in dismay. "They weren't real?"

His mother laughed. "No," she said. "Samuel Clemens made them up."

"But there were a lot of boys who lived along the Mississippi River just like that," said Dad. "Still are." He looked in the rearview mirror and grinned. "I know a couple of boys who still fit the bill. Little river rogues, that's what they are. And their baby brother will be just like them, I'm certain!"

Sam and Jake grinned at one another. They couldn't wait until their little brother was just a little older so they could teach him all the neat tricks they knew. *If Mom and Dad only knew!*

Sam lay back in his seat and looked out the sunroof of their SUV at the tall trees overhead. It was easy to picture this part of the United States being where so many lumberjacks had once lived. He loved

the tall tales about Paul Bunyan and Babe, the Big Blue Ox. Of course, today, everyone fought to save trees, but back then, when there had been a country to build, "Timber!" was heard throughout the countryside, he imagined.

Sam tried to imagine wearing a plaid shirt, and overalls, and big, thick boots. Then he looked down and saw that he was wearing just that! It would have been great fun to have crosscut contests to see who could saw a tree down the fastest. Or to wear spiked boots and try to stand on logs rolling in the swiftly-moving water.

But right now, as they headed toward Hannibal, he was mostly curious what his friend Christina meant by "a mystery's afoot." Mystery followed Christina around like a little dark cloud. Sometimes, she had told him, it was fun. And other times, it was just plain *scary*.

6 TOO MANY TOMBSTONES

In the middle of the extremely creepy graveyard, Christina bent down and picked up the rose. A thorn stuck her in the finger and a thin stream of blood—just the color of the rose—trickled down her hand.

"Great!" she said aloud to no one. "Just great. That can't be a good omen. Blood—isn't that what vampires drink? But, of course, I don't believe in vampires, do I?"

I vant to drink your blood! a deep voice said behind her, and Christina jumped a foot into the air. She swirled around to see Grant with his jacket held over his shoulders like a cape.

"Grant!" she screeched. "Knock it off. That wasn't funny."

"Seemed funny to me," her brother said. "Come on. Mimi and Papa said we've got to catch the streetcar.

Watcha got?" he added, nodding at the rose.

Christina held the rose out to him. "Apparently—a clue!"

"A clue to what?" asked Grant. "There isn't any mystery going on. This is summer vacation."

"Think not?" said his sister. She sashayed bravely down the walkway toward the entrance to the cemetery. The day was almost over and long shadows fell across the paths like arms and legs of bone. "Then read this!" She thrust the note at her little brother.

Grant caught the note in mid-air. He stopped to read it aloud. "It says:

KEEP AN
EYE OUT FOR
RIVER ROGUES.

Well, what does that mean? We haven't even gotten to see the river yet. So, I don't see . . ."

Suddenly Grant looked up. His sister was not in sight. No one was in sight. The wind caused one tree

limb to grate noisily against another. Grant began to run. "Christina!" he called loudly. "CHRISTINA! WAIT FOR ME!!!!!!!!!!!!!!!"

As they rode the streetcar back downtown, dusk settled into the nooks and crannies and Spanish Moss-covered trees of old New Orleans. The jagged edge of a red sunset seemed to turn the city to the color of blood.

At the end of the line, Papa hurried the tired kids off the streetcar and into a restaurant. Christina was so glad. She was starving. All she wanted was a quiet dinner and to go to bed.

But when the door to Mulate's opened, Grant and Christina gasped. There was a wild party going on. The place was filled with people. The "joint was jumping!" as Mimi said. A gigantic fake (or was it real?) alligator greeted them overhead. A hundred wooden tables covered in red and white checked tablecloths seemed to bounce on their skinny legs to the sound of the noisy music.

Christina could detect the sound of a banjo and a harmonica, but she couldn't imagine what the other instruments could be.

"A squeezebox—an accordion," Papa said, when she asked. "And, that washboard-looking thing is, well, it's a washboard!"

One of the musicians played the rippled tin board like he really was scrubbing clothes. The man on the accordion squeezed it in and out as fast as he could. All the men in the band wore plaid shirts and red suspenders. They sang in twangy voices, the strangest words Christina had ever heard. To her it sounded like:

"Do de dy, crawfish pie, and a fee-lay gumbo...
For tonight I'm gonna see my ma cher a mio
Do de dy, do de dy, and be gay-o,
Tonight we'll have good fun on the bayou!"

All around the wooden dance floor in the center of the restaurant, people young and old, moved up a storm in a festive dance that looked sort of like a polka. The "two-step" Mimi called it.

"What are they saying?" Grant asked, as they took their seats.

"Oh, all that's Cajun for 'let the good times roll!'" said Papa.

He took a menu from a waitress and Christina

begged, "No more mud bugs—please?"

Papa laughed and ordered in a loud voice over the music. "Some seafood gumbo, and some catfish and red beans and rice—family style, please."

Soon, platters of steaming food arrived. The band took a break and in the quiet, Mimi reached over and took Christina's arm. "Did you cut yourself? That looks like blood."

Christina and her brother exchanged guilty glances. "No," Christina said honestly, "I didn't cut myself." Then she added quickly, "Can we eat? I'm starving!"

"Me, too," said Grant. "Bring on the mud bugs and the gator tails! I could eat a bear—hair and all!"

That night Christina slept fitfully. To her, New Orleans seemed like a strange city where it was hard to tell reality from make-believe. She dreamed of masked Mardi Gras paraders, alligators sniffing her toes, a mime screaming at her but making no noise, and tombs with doors creaking open. It was not a good night.

7 THE MIGHTY MISSISSIPPI!

The next morning was bright and sunny. When the taxi driver pulled up to the loading dock for the *Delta Queen*, the kids were disappointed. "So this is the Mississippi River?" said Grant. "It doesn't look so big to me."

They sat in the Cafe du Monde where they gobbled biegnets[5]—small hollow doughnuts coated in powdered sugar—and looked out at the famous river.

"Don't be so sure," said Papa. "See those barges—they're pretty big! Besides, this is just part of the river; you're going to see a lot more of it as we make our way up the Mississippi."

Suddenly the *Delta Queen* pulled into view. Christina gasped. It was beautiful! The famous paddlewheeler looked like a floating wedding cake. She could hardly wait to board.

[5] ben YAYS

"Do I have time to e-mail Sam?" she asked Mimi excitedly.

Mimi slapped her laptop on the table and turned it toward her granddaughter. Quickly Christina typed:

**Boarding D.Q. now; no more clues news.
Meet you in St. Louis. T.**

She hit SEND, then closed the computer and spun it back around to Mimi.

"All aboard that's goin' aboard!" shouted Papa.

"I think that's what you say for a train," said Grant.

"Whatever gets you slowpokes off your feet and headin' for the barn," Papa said and the kids giggled. They didn't understand all Papa said, but they knew when he meant hurry-it-up!

As the *Delta Queen* idled, Christina and Grant crowded around the tour guide on the bow of the boat as she told everyone about the famous Mississippi River. In a chirpy voice, she began her spiel:

"The Mississippi River is the longest river in the United States—almost 4,000 miles long. The Ojibway Indians called it the Missi Sipi, which meant Great River. Its headwaters—or beginning—is actually in Minnesota. However, some of the tributaries that bring water to the Mississippi are as far away as western Montana.

Christopher Columbus may have seen the Mississippi River. But Spanish explorer Hernando de Soto gets credit in the history books for discovering the river. That was way back in 1541. In 1673, French explorers Father Jacques Marquette and Louis Jolliet actually traveled down the river by boat.

A lot of other famous people are associated with the river. You may have heard of the author Mark Twain who wrote about two boys named Tom Sawyer and Huckleberry Finn and their adventures on the Mississippi.

Of course, another famous thing about the river is that it floods. Over the years, a system of locks, dams, dikes, and levees have been built to help avoid flooding. But every few years, there is usually a major flood that breaks through these barriers and lots of water washes over the towns on the banks of the river.

Now, if you'll follow me . . ."

"That's all interesting," Grant said. "But I just got out of school. Let's run back to the end of the boat and look at the big paddlewheels instead."

"I agree!" said Christina. "Race ya!" And off the two kids tore from the bow to the stern of the boat. They had to dodge passengers with a lot of "S'cuse me!" and "Sorry!" The sun had come out and the red and white boat gleamed merrily in the dark water.

When they reached the stern, Grant was the first to hang his head over the railing. "Look!"

"Be careful!" Christina said, then joined him. She leaned over, barely on tiptoe. They watched the enormous paddlewheels churn up the water into a sparkling froth. "Wow! It's beautiful."

"Cool!" Grant said. "I can feel some of the water spray."

Suddenly the two big smokestacks on the ship belched gray smoke and a horn blasted long and low. They were off!

"I hope Sam and Jake are having as much fun getting to St. Louis as we are," Christina said.

Christina felt that all the creepy cemetery mystery was behind her now. Nothing to do but have fun and enjoy her vacation. That was because she had

not noticed that the mime—in a black suit, now talking up a storm to passengers nearby—had also boarded the *Delta Queen*. He talked to a couple of newlyweds, but he watched Christina. *Closely. Very closely.*

8 DOWN THE MISSISSIPPI

Sam, Jake, their parents, and baby brother Luke rode down alongside the Mississippi River for what seemed days on end. It was a pretty ride. Sometimes there were tall bluffs where Sam could imagine Indians and cowboys duking it out in the past.

There was a lot of beautiful pastureland. Dad told them that great herds of buffalo once roamed there. But that was before they were all killed off. Today, there were only a few small buffalo herds. They grazed on private land or in national parks.

The farms along the way looked like pictures out of storybooks Sam and Jake had read when they were younger. The dark, chocolate-colored soil had been tilled into neat rows. The crops of corn and wheat they saw were growing taller as they sped southward. Each morning and afternoon felt a little warmer and sunnier.

Sometimes, Dad crossed a big iron bridge that went over the Mississippi, just so the boys could look up and down the river. They saw long barges loaded with heaps of coal being pushed upstream by fat, little tugboats.

One morning, they even put their car on a little ferry boat and rode across the river, then back. It was then that Sam first felt he understood what it must be like to live on the river—a long time ago, and even today. The feeling gave him goosebumps.

Sam had been so busy looking out the car window, playing cards with Jake, and daydreaming about living alongside the Mississippi, that he had forgotten to worry about Christina's mysterious e-mail.

"Hey, look!" cried Jake suddenly. "Is that an eagle?"

Dad pulled the car off the side of the road and got out the binoculars. After watching for a moment where Jake had pointed, he said, "Sure is! You've got eagle-eyes, buddy."

They all took turns watching the eagle soar lazily back and forth over the river.

"Why don't we stop and have our picnic lunch here?" Mom said.

"I was hoping you'd say that!" said Dad.

"Me, too!" said Sam.

"Me, three!" said Jake.

"Mrmm-thrmm-goo," said baby Luke from the backseat.

They had stopped at what the sign called a "Wayside." It was a beautiful area of green grass and flowering dogwood and redbud trees overlooking the river from a high bluff. Mom led the way to the picnic table closest to the water and spread a red-checkered cloth over it. Dad followed with the picnic basket and thermos jug. Sam and Jake tugged their baby brother out of his carseat.

"Be careful!" Sam warned Luke. "Don't get too close to the edge. You'll fall over."

"Ober?" said Luke, and Sam and Jake just rolled their eyes and sighed.

"I'll take him" said Mom, and Sam and Jake handed off their brother and headed for the table.

Mom had stopped at a roadside diner when the boys were still asleep earlier this morning. The picnic basket was filled with fried chicken, potato salad, baked beans, and fat brownies smothered in chocolate frosting. Dad poured them cold glasses of milk from the

thermos.

"Yum!" said Sam. "This is the best lunch ever! Hey, Dad, while we eat, tell us about life on the river long ago. I wish I had lived here back then."

Dad laughed. "I think you boys might have liked that a lot," he said. "You could get up each morning and put on overalls and a straw hat, and you'd be dressed for the day."

"No shoes?" asked Jake. He preferred velcro to laces.

"Nope," said Dad. "You don't need shoes to go swimming and fishing. Of course you might want to wear shoes to go spelunking."

"Spe-what?" Jake said.

"Spelunking," Sam said. "Cave exploring. I learned that in Scouts."

They all looked out over the Mississippi River valley. "The old days were really something, weren't they, Dad?" Sam said wistfully. He wondered if he'd really like to trade his headphones and Palm Pilot for bare feet and a whole lot of goofing-off. Sounded great at the moment.

Suddenly their Mom burst into laughter. "What's so funny, Becky Thatcher?" Dad asked.

"Just thinking," Mom said. "Thought you boys might want to remember that the old days also included outhouses, corncobs, no heat unless you chopped a lot of wood, no air conditioning, a lot of hot, hard farm chores for some kids, no television or movies, no Internet, no . . ."

"Whoa, Mom!" Sam said. "I think we get your point. I guess the good old days weren't always so great, after all."

"What were the corncobs for?" Jake asked.

Dad laughed. "When you went to the outdoor privy to go to the bathroom, sometimes all you had to wipe your bottom with was corncobs—or maybe some pages from the Sears and Roebuck catalog."

"YUUUUUUUUUUCK!" both boys said together.

"And there were other hardships, too," Dad added. "Like keeping the dikes and levees built up so the river wouldn't flood your home. And then when it did—as it always did—having to clean mud and muck and snakes and rats out of your house so you could live in it again. That is, if your house didn't wash away."

"Wow, Dad," said Sam. "How did you learn all this? Did you live way back then?"

Dad frowned. "No! But I read a lot. Maybe you'd better stick your nose in books more than you do right now. You don't know how fortunate you are to have books at home and at the school library and the Peachtree City library. Back in Tom and Huck's day, most homes only had a Bible, if that."

"Why did you call Mom Becky Thatcher?" Jake asked.

"I do read!" Sam protested. "So I know the answer to that question. Becky was Tom's friend. Only she was sort of a pest to him."

"As he was to her!" Mom said.

"Were they real people?" Jake asked. He was gnawing on his third chicken leg.

"Remember? All those characters were fictional," Mom explained. "Mark Twain made them up. But he did such a good job that even today, we feel like they really lived."

"I guess that's good writing," Sam said.

"I guess we'd better get going," Dad said. His voice sounded nervous. "See those storm clouds brewing to the west? I think a whopper could be headed our way. And this is tornado country, too."

As if proving Dad right, a sudden gust of wind

blew a napkin off the picnic table and whisked it toward the cliff. Without thinking, Jake jumped up and ran to catch it. He knew they shouldn't leave litter behind. But each time he reached the napkin, another gust blew it just out of reach.

Suddenly the rest of the family realized Jake was headed right toward the edge of the steep cliff. "Stop, Jake!" his parents screamed.

Sam took off running after his brother. "Stop, Jake!" he screamed. Just a few feet from the treacherous edge of the cliff, he caught his brother by the arm. "Look!" he cried out.

Down below—waaaaaay down below—the river had been whipped by the wind so that whitecaps like the ocean had flicked in white flashes across the water. Gently, Sam tugged his brother back to safety as the thunder and lightning crept ever closer.

Back in the safety of the car, Dad steered the car back onto the River Road in the pelting rain. Sam snuggled into the backseat and e-mailed Christina:

HAD A CLOSE CALL! HOW ARE YOU DOING?

9 THE DELTA QUEEN

Christina was doing great. She loved the water anyway, so being aboard a boat where you could sightsee both sides of the river right from the top deck was a perfect way to tour the Mississippi, in her way of thinking.

She had lost Grant somewhere along the way, but she knew he couldn't go anywhere but on the boat, so she did not worry about him. Mimi and Papa had settled into their cabin and were sitting on the balcony enjoying iced tea and watching the sights from there.

Christina felt grown up and special just to walk the decks of the majestic *Delta Queen* on her own. Every now and then during her walk, she caught up with one small tour group or another. She tagged along just long enough to learn a new fact or two, then went on her way. Of course, she had no way to know that the

mime was following on her heels.

Back on the bow of the top deck, she stopped to hear one tour guide say:

"Now I know everyone knows about the famous Mississippi River Delta. This is the enormous wedge of land on either side of the river where tons and tons of silt are deposited as the river flows out into the Gulf of Mexico. This silt creates some of the most fertile farmland in the world! The dark black soil is called alluvial because it comes from the tributaries—all the creeks and rivers that flow into the Mississippi.

Of course, the Mississippi does not flow in a straight line like it might look on a map. The river meanders back and forth. To help control the flow of the river—and avoid flooding—the U.S. Army Corps of Engineers often cut passages through some of the land that connects the river's path. This created oxbow or horseshoe-shaped lakes, often used for recreation, like water skiing, these days."

Christina looked ahead and could see that, indeed, the river was going to take a big turn to the left. Let's see, she thought. That would be *port*. *Starboard*

was to the right side. She remembered these nautical terms from boating with Mimi and Papa on their boat, the *My Girl*. It was a nice boat, but it was not the *Delta Queen*, she thought.

As the tour group went on, Christina sat down on a red and white striped deck chair and pulled out her Palm Pilot. She saw that she had a message and soon read that Sam and his family had had a close call. "What could that be all about?" she wondered aloud.

"What be all about?" a man sitting in the next deck chair asked.

Christina turned to look at him. He was pretty young and wore a black suit, which seemed sort of strange on this warm spring afternoon. She thought he looked a little familiar, but since she did not know a single soul in Louisiana except for her family, she knew she could not know the man. So, that made him a stranger, didn't it? And she was not supposed to talk to strangers. Still, he seemed nice, and he was on this boat just like her—just traveling on vacation, she figured. So, she felt safe in talking to him.

"My friends Sam and Jake are somewhere north of St. Louis, Missouri—where we're supposed to meet in a few days," Christina told the man. He smiled at her

as she continued. "My grandmother is going to speak at a conference there about Lewis and Clark's famous exploration trip."

"Oh, I'm a writer, too!" said the man. "Perhaps I know your grandmother. What is her name?"

"Carole Marsh," Christina said proudly. "She's pretty famous, but mostly for kids' books. She writes a lot of mystery books for kids. I help her."

The man was really smiling now, very friendly and eager to talk. He pulled out a small notebook, like any writer might do. "Where are you staying in St. Louis" the man asked. When Christina looked hesitant to answer, he added, "Maybe I can interview your grandmother there. I'm going to St. Louis, too. To write for the newspaper."

Christina knew Mimi liked to be interviewed. She often had her picture in the paper and articles written about her. But Papa did all the travel arrangements, and Christina had no idea where they would be staying.

"Oh, I don't know," she finally answered. The man looked disappointed. "But I know it is a tall hotel near the Gateway Arch because we are supposed to visit the museum there and ride up into the arch, too."

The man smiled once more.

"We'll I've got to go find my little brother," Christina said to the man.

"Yes, you'd better keep an eye on him," the man said. "Wouldn't want the river rogues to get him!" He stretched and rose. Tucking his notebook into his back pocket, he nodded and strolled off.

Christina frowned. He sure was nosy, she thought to herself. And why did he have to mention river rogues? As Christina skipped off the other way, a fleeting thought made her feel a little sick to her stomach. How did he know Mimi was a writer? Hadn't he said that before she had ever mentioned it?

Christina couldn't remember the order of their conversation that clearly, so she just shrugged and skipped on. It was too pretty a day to worry about a man she'd never met before. Still, maybe she'd better go look for her brother.

As Christina sashayed across the second deck, someone whistled at her. "Over here!"

It was Grant. Christina was actually glad to see him. Her imagination had gone a little wild after her

conversation with the man. She knew Grant could be anywhere, but could he have fallen overboard?

"We should stick together, Grant," she said when they met at the starboard railing.

"Why?" Grant asked. His big, blue eyes looked up at her. Christina shook her silky, brown hair back and forth. "Just because!" she said. Her brother just shrugged.

"Hey, I heard from Sam," Christina shared. "He said they'd had a close call, but he didn't say what it was."

Grant went into one of his funny wild and crazy tirades. First he rose up tall with his arms outstretched overhead. "Maybe they were attacked by zeuglodons! Those were big, whalelike dinosaurs. They could still be hiding in the river!"

Next Grant flopped down on his belly and stuck his arms out to make a giant chomping jaw. "Or maybe they were 'et' by alligators. There are a few of them in the river. A few hundred!"

As Christina giggled, Grant then began to prance back and forth with his hands on his little hips. "Or maybe the pirates got them. River pirates!" He had a pretend duel with a pretend sword.

Now Christina was laughing out loud. People passing by steered around the two children. A couple of kids tugged at their parents' arms, straining to see what the noisy boy was up to.

"Cut out all the dramatics," Christina urged her brother. "You're starting to attract attention. You are such a big ham!" she teased.

"I'm not a ham!" Grant protested. "I'm not even a pork chop. Or bacon. Or sausage. Or . . ."

Suddenly Grant was interrupted by the deep voice of Papa. "Or anywhere to be seen!" he groused. "Mimi is waiting for us in the dining room," he told his grandchildren. "It is time for dinner, you little river rogues!"

Would everybody quit saying that, Christina thought to herself as she followed Papa, who had Grant the Gator tucked up under one arm, to the dining room of the *Delta Queen*.

10 RIVER ROGUES

Mimi waved merrily as they entered the amazing dining room. She was all the way across the room, seated at a table looking out a window where you could watch the river go by (or was it you go by the river?) while they ate.

Mimi wore a white dress and a straw hat with a wide brim that had a red and white striped ribbon around it. She matched the dining room, which was beautiful with white tablecloths, silver teapots, white candles, and red and white striped chairs.

When they got to the table, Papa plunked Grant down into one chair. Then he pulled out another chair and let Christina sit down. Her grandfather was such a gentleman! Next Papa sat down and a waiter immediately appeared and poured ice water.

"I hope you kids have been having fun and being

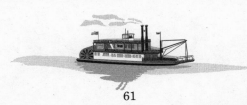

careful," Mimi said. "I had a nice nap in a chair on the upper deck. Then I went to write, but I couldn't find my computer. I wanted to work on my speech."

"Oh, it's probably not unpacked yet," Papa said. "I took a nap, too. I'll look for it after dinner."

As the waiter set down their plates, Christina looked out the window at the river. The sun was beginning to go down and an eerie red cast made the water look bloody. The green trees on the bank were now tall, black silhouettes. The river that looked so cheerful and inviting in the daylight seemed to be turning into a spooky place as night came on.

As they ate catfish and hushpuppies and cole slaw, the dining room buzzed with soft conversation. The light of hundreds of white candles in hurricane lamps flickered in reflections in the windows, making the river look alive with floating light.

"Papa," Christina began. "Are there really anything called river rogues on the Mississippi?" She thought her grandfather would laugh and tease her for such a thought, so she was surprised at his answer.

"Absolutely!" Papa said. "In fact, right along the area we're passing now was once infested with

river rogues." Papa checked his map. "Yep! This area of the Mississippi River was known as Under-the-Hill. Rough and rowdy men drank and gambled in the caves just beneath the city of Natchez. Some were ordinary rivermen. They ran the flatboats, pirogues, barges, and keelboats up and down the river. But others were greedy and eager and mean. They became real river pirates, who'd rather rob and kill than work to get ahead."

"That sounds like the wild, wild West!" Grant said.

"It was!" said Mimi. "Remember, America was still a young country. The Mississippi and the West were just being discovered. People had often left hard, poor lives to try to find better lives. Only they often found even harder lives."

"And they had weapons," Papa added. "Back then, men walked around with knives, pistols, and they knew how to fight with their fists. It was rough."

"Like Jim Bowie?" Grant asked. "Didn't he invent the Bowie knife?"

"Yes," said Mimi. "And people still fought duels, although it was ordinary fisticuffs that left most men bloodied and broke after being robbed."

"If you were caught, you might be hanged," Papa said.

"Wow!" said Christina. "No wonder people talk about river rogues."

"Was someone talking to you about river rogues?" Mimi asked.

Christina ducked her head and began to eat faster. "No, not really," she said.

"Well, both you kids just remember that we still have con artists today, so be careful who you talk to," Mimi warned.

"We know—don't talk to strangers," Grant said, bored.

Christina didn't say a word. She sure wasn't going to mention a stranger she had talked to just this day, especially a stranger that talked about river rogues. She just looked thoughtfully out the window and wondered was was going on on the riverbank in the darkness.

The waiter appeared and cleared their plates. Then he brought dessert—chocolate cheesecake. Each white plate was drizzled with raspberry sauce. And Christina's plate had a red rose on it. And a white note.

11 TOM SAWYER AND HUCKLEBERRY FINN

Sam and Jake were excited to finally be in Hannibal, Missouri. It was still stormy, but they wore bright yellow slickers and rainboots. Luke was asleep in the carseat. Mom said she would stay with him while Dad took the boys to see the famous cave where Tom Sawyer and Huckleberry Finn were said to have hung out.

"Mark Twain lived here as a boy," Mom said. "His real name was Samuel Langhorne Clemens. He wrote about Tom and Huck."

"So why didn't he use his real name?" Jake asked.

"Some writers write under a fake name," Sam said.

"That's right," said Mom. "It's called a pseudonym[6] or a pen name."

[6] SUE doe nim

"I think I'd like to have a pen name," said Jake. "Then if I did something bad, I could say, 'That wasn't me—it was John.'"

"That's not really the purpose of a pen name," Mom said.

"Tell them what Mark Twain's pen name meant," Dad said.

Mom laughed. "He got his pen name by using the term that meant measuring the depth of the water. As you measured, you'd call back to the captain of the boat, 'MARK TWAIN!'"

"That sounds silly," said Sam.

"Well it wasn't," said Dad. "You sure didn't want to run your boat aground on a shallow sandbar."

"And you didn't want to get struck by any snags or sawyers," Mom added.

"What are those?" Jake asked.

"Stuff in the water," said Sam. "There's a lot of junk in the water today," he noted. He pointed to a large log floating rapidly downstream.

"That's because of the storm," Dad said. "The water is high, and it's brought a lot of debris on the riverbanks down into the river. If your boat hit a log like that it could cause you to sink."

"Good thing we're in an SUV," said Jake.

"Good thing we're on dry land," said Sam.

"Come on, boys," said Dad. He opened the door and the boys hopped out into a mud puddle. "We'll be right back," Dad told their mother. "We just want to take a peek at the famous cave."

Their mother sat quietly in the car as little Luke snored in the backseat. She read a book for awhile, then laid her head back for a short nap of peace and quiet.

In the meantime, Sam and Jake ran ahead of Dad. The boys ran into the cave for a short ways, then stopped dead cold.

"Will this help?" Dad called from behind them. He clicked on a large flashlight and spewed the light around the entrance to the cave.

The dark cave seemed to gobble up the light like a giant mouth. Sam wondered if he was seeing bats hanging upside down over there in the corner. The cave was damp and chilly. It was slimy beneath their

feet. It was really spooky and scary. Soon the boys slowed down.

Dad caught up and laughed. "Had enough?"

"For now," said Sam, nonchalantly, as if he'd keep going.

"Not me," said Jake. "Let's keep going." He marched ahead.

Suddenly, the flashlight flickered off.

"Hey, Dad!" called Jake. "Where are you guys?"

"Over here!" Sam called to his brother.

"Where's that?" Jake said. There was a whimper in his voice.

Suddenly, something grabbed Jake by the arm. "Let's go, spelunker!" his Dad said. Holding his sons' hands, he slowly led them out of the cave into the gray daylight.

When they got back to the car, they could see their mother looking out of the car window with a frantic look on her face. The SUV was surrounded by water! The river had flooded the riverbank and washed around the car.

"Stay here, boys!" Dad shouted, and they knew

Aaaaahhhh! Bats!!

he meant business. The boys clung to one another. Dad ran to the car. The water sloshed around his ankles. He opened the back door, then returned to grab each boy and toss them in the car. By the time he got inside, the water was almost above the tires.

Quickly, Dad started the engine. He slowly drove the car away from the river and up a concrete ramp to the ferry landing. "Are you still going?" he called to the ferryman.

"Last trip!" the man called back. He waved for them to drive onto the flat metal ferryboat.

"I'm not too sure about this," Mom said.

"It'll be okay," said Dad.

As soon as their car was on board, the man hooked a chain across the end of the ferry, and the engine started. Slowly they pulled away from the dock. The ferryboat rocked and rolled as if it were dancing its way across the river.

"Where are we headed?" Mom asked. "The dock is over there, but we're headed the other direction."

"That's because of the strong current," Dad said. "He has to go against the current to get where he's going. I hope he knows what he is doing!"

Everyone held their breath as the ferry slowly chugged toward the landing on the opposite shore. Just when it seemed they would miss the dock and go sputtering downstream at the mercy of the river, the ferryman gunned the engine. A man on the dock tossed a thick rope over the railing of the ferryboat. A deckhand tied it tight.

As soon as the chain on that end of the ferryboat was removed, Dad started the engine and drove onto the concrete boat ramp. The ramp was already half under water and the river was rising faster and faster.

"Thanks!" called Dad out the window into the rain. The ferryman just nodded. Rain dripped down his face, nose, and chin.

When they got back up on the River Road, Mom let out a big sigh. "Let's get on to St. Louis," she said. "I can't wait to tell Mimi about our big river adventures."

In the backseat, Jake was so relieved to be out of the cave and across the river, he had fallen asleep from exhaustion. Sam snuck Dad's Palm Pilot out of his backpack and typed, then sent this message to Christina:

WE'RE HAVING ADVENTURES! HOW ABOUT YOU?

12 EARTHQUAKE?!

Just before she went to bed, Christina checked her Palm Pilot.

WE'RE HAVING ADVENTURES!
HOW ABOUT YOU?

Sam had e-mailed her. "Not really," Christina said to herself. Then she thought, we're having fun—and maybe a little mystery—but not really any adventure yet. She felt a little jealous.

Of course, Sam and his family were heading south to St. Louis by car. She and her family were on this neat boat. She wondered what kind of adventure Sam was having: fun adventure or scary adventure. She guessed she'd have to wait to find out.

Just before she fell asleep, she placed the rose

that she had gotten on her dessert plate at dinner on the table beside her bed. She opened the note and read it for the third time. It said:

JEAN LAFITTE
HAD BIG FEET.
DON'T BE A
RAT FINK!

    Papa had laughed when she read it aloud at the table. He told them that Jean Lafitte had been a pirate in Louisiana a long time ago. Also, he said that Mike Fink had been the "King of the Keelboatmen." He was said to be the strongest man in the world at that time.

    But none of that information helped Christina figure out what the clue meant. Grant had no idea either. Mimi and Papa wondered why she had gotten a note from anyone at all. Christina was saved from giving an explanation when a man with a banjo appeared at their table and played a couple of jazzy tunes for

them. By the time he finished, her grandparents had forgotten about the note, which she had quickly tucked into her pocket.

Just as Christina fell asleep, she heard Mimi complaining in the other room that she still could not find her computer. Papa promised he would look again in the morning.

The next morning it was raining and foggy. Mimi was grouchy because her computer was nowhere to be seen. Papa was in trouble because he couldn't find it. Grant was still asleep.

Papa put on his raincoat and Christina did the same. They grabbed a couple of red and white striped umbrellas from a holder beside their cabin door and went outside into the drizzle.

"Where are we now?" Christina asked. They stood near the starboard railing. Papa sipped his coffee; Christina slurped her hot chocolate. Papa checked his map, trying not to get it wet.

"We're at New Madrid, Missouri," Papa said. "This is the place that once had an earthquake bigger than the famous San Francisco earthquake."

"Wow!" said Christina. "I thought that was the biggest earthquake of all—and it started a fire, too."

"In 1811 and 1812, three gigantic earthquakes rumbled New Madrid," Papa said. "They were so strong that they shook the ground like someone holding onto the edge of a blanket. It shook the earth for hundreds and hundreds of miles. Damage to sidewalks and buildings occurred as far away as Boston, Massachusetts!"

"They don't have earthquakes around here anymore, do they?" Christina asked nervously.

"Oh, they expect a real whopper most anytime," said Papa. "The geologists say this area is overdue for another big quake."

Suddenly, the boat began to quiver and shake! An earthquake, Christina wondered? An EARTHQUAKE? But a deckhand ran passed them and shouted, "Just a little run-aground! We'll be off in a minute."

Christina and Papa laughed in relief. Grant stormed out of their cabin and said, "Did you feel that?!"

Mimi was right behind them. "What was that? An earthquake?!" she asked.

Papa gave Christina a wink. Together they looked at Mimi and Grant with innocent faces.

"What was what?" Christina asked.

"I didn't feel a thing," Papa said with a shrug.

Grant and Mimi stormed back into the cabin. And Christina and Papa laughed so hard their sides hurt.

13 THE GATEWAY ARCH

They got to St. Louis at dusk. The sunset over the Mississippi River was as red as fire. The gigantic Gateway Arch looked black against the sky. Sam thought it was so cool. He could not imagine how someone ever built the arch. But his Dad told them about it as they crossed the river.

"It's really stainless steel," he told the boys. That unusual shape is called a catenary curve. It rises 630 feet above the ground!"

"Wow!" said Jake. "And we get to go up in it?"

"When Christina and Grant get here tomorrow," Mom reminded them.

"What's the arch for?" Sam asked.

"It was built in honor of the pioneers, explorers, fur trappers, gold miners, hunters, soldiers, missionaries, and other people who helped open the

wilderness west of the Mississippi River," said Dad.
"The land where the arch sits was once a famous
trading post."

"Did everybody come in those big, old, covered
wagons?" Jake asked.

"They came any way they could!" Dad said. "On
foot, horseback, wagon train—and of course many of
them crossed the Mississippi River to get here—just like
we're doing tonight."

"It was a looooooong way," said Mom. "But you
know, when they got to St. Louis, their journey had
really just begun. They still had a long way to go to get
to the gold fields, or the great plains where they built
sod houses, or anywhere else west they were headed."

"Just like Little House on the Prairie?" Jake
asked.

"Lots of those little houses blew away!" Sam
said. "We studied it in school. They cut down all the
trees and the land turned into dust. Then the wind
whipped up the dust and they couldn't grow crops
anymore. So they were poor. And there was the Great
Depression and a lot of people were out of work. Some
starved to death."

"Is that true, Dad?" Jake asked, not quite

believing his brother, even though he was smart in school and made all "A"s.

"Sure is," said Dad.

"Then those weren't really the good old days, were they?" said Mom. "No school or only a little one-room school house to attend. And no school bus. You had to walk for miles, even in the snow. And you might not even have any shoes to wear. And no vaccines like we have today so people got sick real easy. It was a hard life."

The boys sat back in their seats and watched the Gateway Arch. It was pretty amazing. But so was the story of all the people who were brave enough to come west, they thought. Jake wished their SUV was really a Conestoga wagon. Sam was glad they were headed to a nice hotel . . . and not a house made out of dirt!

The next morning at the hotel, the boys were excited since Christina and Grant would be here before lunch time. Jake and Luke watched cartoons. Sam had found a book about the Gateway Arch and some paper in a drawer.

"What are you doing?" Mom asked Sam. She

was unpacking. Sam looked up from the desk where he sat. He could look right out and see the arch. "I'm writing a report," he said. "Maybe I can use it in school for extra credit next year."

His mother stopped and watched Sam writing neatly on the paper. "But Sam," she said suddenly, "you're copying the book word for word."

"Yeah, I know," said Sam. He looked up at his mother. "What's wrong with that?"

"When you copy someone else's writing word-for-word, that's like stealing their words. That's called plagiarism[7]. It's illegal."

"Then how do I write about the arch if I don't know anything but what I read?" Sam asked.

"You can read that book for research and use it for a reference tool," Mom explained. "But then you should write what you have learned in your own words— not copy someone else's."

"Oh," Sam said. "I never thought about it that way. I guess Christina's grandmother would be upset if someone copied her stories and put their name on it."

"Wouldn't you?" Mom asked.

"I sure would," Sam said. "Okay, I'm going to start over, but I better get an A."

[7] PLAY juh rizm

Mom rubbed her son's hair. "Maybe your paper will be even better than the stuff you're reading!" she said.

"Maybe so," said Sam. "What I'm reading is pretty dull."

"Well, you make it exciting—just like the past really was," Mom said. "Maybe you can grow up and become a writer?"

Sam grinned. "Maybe—if I get a computer for Christmas!" he hinted.

When Mom went back to unpacking, Sam stopped to check for e-mails. Christina had sent him the following message:

EARTHQUAKE! RIVER ROGUES! ROSES! SEE YA SOON!!

14 MEET ME IN ST. LOUIE, LOUIE!

As they bounced down the gangplank of the *Delta Queen*, Grant and Papa walked arm in arm. As loudly as they could, they sang, *"Old Man River . . . that Old Man River . . . he just keeps rollin' alonnnnnnng!"*

"We don't know them, do we, Mimi?" Christina asked.

"Never saw those gentlemen before in my life," Mimi agreed with a twinkle in her eye.

However, at the bottom of the gangplank, they were more than happy to let Papa handle the luggage. Mimi's computer case sat on top of the stack of suitcases. Her computer had finally shown up—right where she had looked many times before, she insisted. She was sorry that she had lost so much writing time. And, a diskette seemed to be missing. But she was so happy to have her computer back, she let the matter

drop.

As they stood on the dock waiting for a taxi, Papa said, "Well, here we are in St. Louis. Too bad the World's Fair's still not going on!"

"What World's Fair?" Christina asked. Her Uncle Michael had told her all about going to a World's Fair one time. He said it was really neat. Mimi had written a mystery book about it and a trivia book. Of course, Uncle Michael was just a little kid back then. Now Christina and Grant had replaced him as "main characters" in Mimi's books.

"In 1904, St. Louis hosted a World's Fair," Papa said. "It celebrated the 100th anniversary of the signing of the Louisiana Purchase, when the United States bought most of western America from France for about 4 cents an acre."

"What a deal!" Grant said.

"That's what I said!" said Mimi.

"Why do people go to a World's Fair?" asked Christina.

"Mostly for fun and to see all the newfangled things of the era," said Mimi.

"The fair's official name was the Louisiana Purchase Exposition," Papa said. "People who visited saw

wondrous things like electricity and ice cream cones."

"Those were new back then?" Grant asked.

"Sure were," Papa said. "They even wrote a song just for the fair."

"Oh, nooooooo," Mimi and Christina groaned together.

Sure enough, Papa and Grant hooked arms once more and sang—loudly, of course:

> *"Meet me in St. Louie, Louie*
> *Meet me at the fair!*
> *I will do the hoochie-koochie . . ."*

That made-up chorus not only made Christina and Mimi laugh, but all those around them who were listening too. Fortunately, about that time the taxi pulled up. They all piled in as the poor taxi driver stuffed all their luggage in the trunk.

As they drove off, Christina never noticed that they were followed by another taxicab. The only passenger was a man in a black suit. Just before he had gotten into the cab, he had bought one dozen red roses from a vendor at the dock.

At the hotel, Sam and Jake were waiting for them in the lobby. Papa had called their Dad on his cell phone to tell them they were en route[8] and their ETA[9] was only ten minutes.

"Hey!

"Hi!!"

"Yeah! You're here!!!"

"Great to see you!!!!"

That's what it was like—plus hugs and kisses all around—for the next ten minutes. Then the adults gravitated off to a comfortable lounge area for coffee and catch-up conversation. Jake and Grant plopped down on the carpet to play with Luke. That gave Christina and Sam a chance to go to the snack bar and catch up.

They went through the line, ordered milkshakes, and sat in a corner booth.

"Got all your e-mails," Sam said. "What's all this about river rogues and roses?"

"I'm not sure," said Christina. "I could have sworn a man in a black suit had been following us, but I haven't seen him since we got off the boat. And I don't know what the clues mean. Or even if they

[8] AHN root; French for on the way
[9] ETA = Estimated Time of Arrival

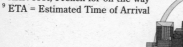

mean anything. The only mystery I've gotten wind of was Mimi's vanished computer, and she found it— only a disk was missing. What about all your ADVENTURE e-mails?"

"Wow!" said Sam. "We almost got lost in a cave, and we almost drowned the car in the river during a flood."

"Well, I thought we were in an earthquake this morning," Christina said. "But the boat had just run aground."

Both kids were quiet for a few minutes. Finally Sam said, teasingly, "So no mystery this trip, hey?"

Christina shook her head. "Well, I don't know. Except for those roses and clues, seems like all is quiet. Maybe we can just sit by the pool or something?"

"That would be fun!" Sam said. "I'm tired of riding in the car. Maybe there's a ball game in town, or something."

As they continued thinking of fun—non-mysterious things to do—Papa stuck his head in the door, "Time to get dressed for lunch!" he said.

Christina had forgotten that they were all

supposed to go to a special lunch at the Museum of Westward Expansion. The museum was located in the basement beneath the giant Gateway Arch. The luncheon was the kick-off celebration for a week of special events related to the famous Lewis and Clark Expedition. Mimi was supposed to give a speech tomorrow night. That was what she had been writing about so hard during their trip.

On the 25th floor of the hotel, their rooms were side by side. They both looked out at the arch. It almost seemed like they could touch it from here. While the adults got dressed, the kids sat in the hallway and watched Luke run up and down, playing peek-a-boo and peep-eye.

When the adults were ready, they took the baby and went downstairs. Christina and Grant headed to their room to get dressed. Sam and Jake opened the door to their room.

"Meet out here in ten minutes," said Sam.

"Make that a hundred minutes for Christina!" said Grant.

"I know how to spell Mississippi," Jake said proudly. Then he began to spell: M I CROOKED LETTER CROOKED LETTER I CROOKED LETTER

CROOKED LETTER I HUMPBACK HUMPBACK I!"

The other kids laughed at him. "Well, I know how to keep time," Grant said. "One Mississippi, two Mississippi, three Mississippi, four Mississippi, five Mississippi, six . . ."

"Okay, Grant!" said Christina. "We get the idea. Let's get dressed, or we will Miss-issippi the whole luncheon."

With that the kids scattered to their rooms. In their room, Grant claimed the bathroom first, slamming the door behind him. Christina grumbled, "Hurry up!" She sat on the bed, waiting her turn, when there was a knock on the door.

Without thinking, Christina opened the door. "Room service!" the man said. He hurried inside and set a silver tray on the table. The tray was covered with a silver dome. "Sign here!"

Christina signed her name on the dotted line beside their room number. "Thank you!" the man said, then hurriedly left, letting the heavy door slam behind him.

Why would we order room service if we're going out to lunch, Christina wondered. Curious, she removed the silver dome from the tray. There on a

white paper doily was a red rose. Beside it lay a note.

Christina gasped. Not again! She sniffed the rose. Then she picked up the note. Was it a clue? A practical joke? Maybe Sam had sent this, now that she had told him about the other clues. After all, no one else knew.

But when she read the note she knew Sam had not sent it. No one nice had sent it, that was for sure.

15 WESTWARD HO!

The Museum of Westward Expansion was quite a museum. They had about an hour before the luncheon started, and everyone took time to look around the incredible array of exhibits.

As Christina wandered from display to display in the exhibit hall, she learned:

- One of the early Indian tribes here was called the Oumes-sourit or "Big Canoe People."
- Once the people had a vote to decide whether to pronounce the state name Missour-ah or Missour-ee, and Missour-ee won out.
- Missouri's nickname is the "Show Me State." It means that you really have to work hard to prove something to Missourians.

•Nomadic hunters and moundbuilders once lived here.

But the most interesting part of the museum was devoted to the story of Meriwether Lewis and William Clark and their famous Corps of Discovery expedition. This was when President Thomas Jefferson sent the two men on a three-year trek out into the unknown western wilderness. They saw many incredible things and reported all of them back to the president. People were pretty amazed at their stories of Indians and buffalo and wild rivers and land, land, land all the way to the Pacific Ocean.

"Hey, look at this picture!" Sam said. He had caught up with Christina at the start of the Mississippi River exhibit.

Christina turned to look at a photograph of a man floating down the river during a flood. Two large rats perched on each of his shoulders.

"Yuck!" said Christina. "I would die if that happened to me."

Sam just shook his head. "Well I guess the poor

rats were trying to save themselves, too."

"Speaking of saving someone," Christina whispered. "I got another clue. It was delivered by room service!"

"What did it say?" Sam asked.

"It said: YOUR MIMI IS A GONER!"

"Hey," said Sam. "That sounds scary. Maybe it's time you told your grandparents about the clues. Maybe they can help."

"Not quite yet," Christina insisted. "They would probably think something dangerous was going on and make all us kids sit in the hotel room and miss all the festivities. No way! Besides, I may figure it out yet."

"But not too late, I hope," Sam said. He saw his Dad waving for him in front of the bookstore and ran off to meet him.

Then Papa appeared in the doorway and called to Christina. She ran to him. "Time for lunch," he said.

The luncheon was held in a gigantic room with what looked like hundreds of round tables covered in white tablecloths. Each table was numbered. They got to sit at table number one because Mimi was a special

guest. That made Christina feel special. She was glad she had worn her new white pants and black and white polka dot shirt. Mimi had put her hair up in pigtails with black and white ribbons. Even Grant looked pretty neat, although his shirt was not tucked into his pants as usual.

Sam and his family sat at table number 13. Christina was glad that was not her table—she just hated the number 13!

"Are you ready to give your speech tonight?" Papa asked Mimi.

"Almost," said Mimi. "I still have a little to write."

"Well, you'd better hurry up," Papa said. "That's just a few hours away and we have to go ride up in the arch before then."

Mimi sighed. "Oh, I don't think I'll have time for that," she said.

"Mimi!" said Christina, "you have to. That is one of the big fun things we came to do."

"Yeah," said Grant. "It won't be any fun without you!"

Mimi laughed and blushed. "Okay, okay, you little hooligans, you've convinced me. I'll go up in the

Gateway Arch with you."

While they were talking and eating, the mistress of ceremonies told all about the evening activities. She introduced Mimi as the main speaker, and she stood up and took a bow. Then she talked about the special passes to ride up into the arch. And about the fireworks show over the Mississippi River afterwards.

Then she introduced the lunch entertainment.

"For your pleasure, we have Mr. Mystery to perform for us this afternoon. He has come all the way from New Orleans via the Delta Queen. Please give him your attention and a round of applause!"

Christina was stunned when the performer appeared out from behind a black curtain. He was a mime! He wore black pants and a red and white striped top and white gloves.

"Mimi!" Christina hissed under her breath. "Isn't that the same mime we saw perform in Jackson Square the other day?"

Mimi laughed. "Oh, Christina, all mimes dress that way. It's part of their act. That could be the man we saw, but I'll bet it's someone completely different.

Shh now, and watch!"

Christina didn't see why she should be quiet. There was nothing to hear. The mime, like all mimes, never spoke a word. He acted out silly stories using props like a stool, a stuffed dog, and a vase of red roses.

Sometimes he acted sad, and the audience went *"Awwwwwww."* Other times, he acted silly, and the audience went *"Haaaaaaaa!"* Then, he'd do a magic trick and the audience went, *"Ohhhhhhhhh!"*

Christina was focused on her ice cream sundae dessert when the mime jumped off the stage and began to wander through the audience. She looked up just in time to see the mime begin to present one of the red roses to Mimi. Then he suddenly winked and turned and handed it to Christina instead. Everyone applauded, but Christina just frowned. She looked but there was no note. Oh, oops, yes, here it was—tucked down in a rosebud. As everyone else continued to watch the mime and laugh and applaud, she slipped the note out and read it. One word, or rather one number:

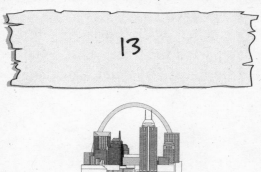

16 ARCH ENEMY

After lunch, the adults and baby Luke went to take a nap to rest up for the festive evening. Sam and Jake had to rest for awhile, too, even if that just meant sitting around and reading, their parents said.

Grant and Papa went for a walk. Papa said exercise gave him more energy that just sitting around.

Mimi sat in front of her computer and pecked at her speech for that night.

Christina sat nearby in a big, overstuffed armchair with a notepad and pen. She thought maybe she could figure out all the rose and river rogue clues. And, if the mime was behind them. And, what the mystery was. But she had no luck and soon dozed off.

While she was sleeping, Christina dreamed that she was bumping along in a covered wagon. Papa was driving, and Mimi was in charge of the chuckwagon.

Grant was just a baby in her dream. They crossed the Mississippi River, keeping a lookout for Indians. Papa said they were going to be sodbusters. Mimi held a shotgun across her lap. Grant kept singing silly songs in the back of the wagon. A man in a black suit with white gloves rode on a horse beside them.

Christina woke up with a start. Mimi had covered her with a blanket and the fringe was tickling her nose. In her dream, it was locusts— eating up all their crops. Christina decided that she was glad she had not been a pioneer girl. She liked the modern world.

While Mimi continued to type, Christina checked her Palm Pilot and found a message from Sam.

MEET ME IN THE HALLWAY BY THE ELEVATOR

"Mimi, can I go down to the snack bar for awhile?" Christina asked. She stretched and yawned, pushing the fringed blanket to the floor.

"Sure," Mimi said absentmindedly. "Bring us back a couple of bottles of water, please."

"Okay," Christina said. She picked the room key

up off the table and put it in her pocket. Then she slipped out the door.

Sam was waiting for her by the elevator.

"I have to go to the snack bar," Christina told him. "Make sure I don't forget to bring back some water."

Sam shrugged and pushed the elevator button for DOWN. "I just wondered if you figured out any of the clues?"

As they boarded the empty elevator, Christina shook her head. "No," she said, as the doors closed. "I tried, but all that brainstorming just put me to sleep."

"It's a mystery to me too," Sam said. He leaned back against the elevator wall. It was a glass-walled elevator, and they could look up through a skylight overhead and down to the lobby below.

"Hey, look!" Christina said suddenly. "See that man down there in the lobby? Isn't he wearing a red and white striped shirt?"

Sam peered downward. "Yes," he finally said. "But he's also selling popcorn. That's just his vendor's uniform."

"Oh," Christina said in disappointment. "I was hoping for something to happen to help me figure this out."

"I was hoping for this elevator to go somewhere," Sam grumbled. "I don't think we've moved at all." He pushed the button for the lobby again and when nothing happened he pushed a bunch of buttons.

"Stop!" Christina warned. "You'll get the elevator all messed up and it won't go anywhere." But just as she said that, the elevator began to move downward. It stopped far above the lobby.

When the door opened, they walked out. It was the 13th floor. They found themselves standing in front of room 1313. And there were a dozen red roses in a glass vase sitting beside the door.

17 RED ROSES FOR A BLUE LADY

Christina and Sam charged back onto the elevator and quickly pushed the LOBBY button hard. The elevator door closed, and they sunk downward. When the door opened in the lobby, they ran headfirst into Grant and Papa.

"Going up?" Papa said cheerfully.

"Going to the snack bar," Christina said grumpily. "Bringing Mimi some water."

"Well, hurry right along and don't take any shortcuts," Papa said. "We're going to the arch in a few minutes."

"Okay," Christina promised, then ducked beneath Papa's arm and ran for the snack bar, Sam chasing after her.

107

"Wow! Look at this thing!" Grant said. He was stretched so far backward, straining up to look at the Gateway Arch overhead, that he almost did a backbend.

"It's so cool," Christina agreed. "It's like an elevator to the sky."

It was a beautiful evening on the grassy area beneath the arch beside the Mississippi River. As the lights slowly winked on in the skyscrapers and on the bridges around the city, St. Louis looked magical, Christina thought. No wonder people had once thought this was a great place to hold a World's Fair.

People milled around, most looking up at the arch. A long line formed in front of the booth where they could buy tickets to go up in the arch.

"Aren't we going to get in line?" Christina asked. "We'll never get to ride."

"Oh we don't need to have a ticket," Mimi said. She pulled four blue passes from her purse. "We have special VIP passes. First we get a tour to see how the arch was built, then we get on a special car to go up. We have about one hour before I have to give my talk."

"Then we'd better get a move on!" Papa said, herding them toward one leg of the arch.

Christina looked around wistfully for Sam and his

family. They had disappeared into the crowd. Probably already getting to ride, Christina thought. Well, she'd see them at the dinner that night. They were all going to sit at the same table. Mimi had arranged it.

At the big door at the entrance to the arch, they were met by a nice young man who had an official GATEWAY ARCH sticker on the lapel of his jacket.

"Hi, I'm Tom!" he said and shook their hands. "I'll give you a brief tour, then we'll go up." Mimi nodded, and the young man continued.

"The Arch is an engineering marvel. At first it was hard to figure out how to devise a transportation system to take people up the legs of the Arch to the top. Then the engineers decided to use a combination of ideas based on elevators, escalators, and the Ferris wheel."

"The Ferris wheel?" Christina interrupted. She was not a big fan of Ferris wheels, so she didn't like the idea that the arch was modeled after one.

"That's right!" Tom continued. "And it worked great. The little capsules you ride in—we call them trams—go sort of up and over the tracks until they reach the top of the Arch. The trip takes four minutes to go up. Then you get out and have to climb a few steps to

the observation deck where you can see for miles and miles and miles.

"Of course, you could walk up the 1,076-step spiral staircase to the top, if you wish," Tom teased.

"No thanks!" said Mimi. "Not in these heels!" She picked up her foot to show off her new red, strappy shoes.

"Does the arch sway in the wind?" Grant asked.

"Yes," said Tom. "But it was made to sway a few inches in each direction—without toppling over, of course!"

"Lightning?" asked Christina. "Does it ever get struck by lightning?"

"It does," Tom admitted. "But the Arch has lightning rods, so it doesn't hurt anything."

"I just have one question," said Papa.

"Yes, sir," Tom said politely. "What is it?"

"When can we go up?" Papa said.

"How about right now?" Tom asked, and the kids cheered.

Christina was a little nervous as they climbed into the tiny capsules. There was only room for five

people, and when they were all inside, they were "snug as a bug in a rug" as Papa often said.

At first everything was still and quiet.

"Glad I don't have Santa Claustrophobia," Grant said.

"That's just claustrophobia, silly," Christina told her brother. Actually, she was the one who was not so crazy about being confined in small, enclosed spaces. But she tried not to think about that right now.

Soon, the car lurched and swung and started slowly upward. It was hard to tell how fast they were going, but every now and then they passed a small window in the leg where they could see outside. Christina thought it was funny that they were all so quiet, sort of like people were on an elevator. She sure hoped Grant and Papa didn't decided to start singing.

Suddenly, the car came to a stop. Tom opened the little door, and they all climbed out to a set of stairs that they had to go up to get to the top of the arch.

Christina was amazed. Instead of being small and tight like she had expected, the top of the arch was actually a very large, long room. On each side were rows of windows where you could look out and seem to see forever.

"What a beautiful sight!" Mimi exclaimed.

"Everyone in America should get to come up here," Papa said. "It's like climbing the Statue of Liberty or the Washington Monument."

"Actually," Tom said, "the Gateway Arch is taller than either one of them!"

"Wow!" they all said together, taking in the magical view.

Nearby, another tourist was also enjoying the view. The view out the windows, and, the view of the family nearby. He wore a black suit—only this time, it was a tuxedo. He kept fiddling with his bow tie as if he was not used to wearing one. When the family moved, he moved, just to stay within a few feet of them. He wore a red rose in his lapel.

What a view!

18 DISASTER STRIKES!

They walked around a little while, then Mimi glanced down at her Carole Marsh Mysteries watch. "Ohmigoodness!" she said. "We have to go. I can't be late for my speech! Can you help us, Tom?"

Tom looked around. "Yes," he said. "I can get you back on a car going down, but I have to stay here to meet my next VIP tour. Do you mind?"

"Not at all," Mimi insisted. "Not as long as we get on out of here. It's wonderful, but I have a speech to give in . . ." She stopped to look at her watch. "In less than 20 minutes."

Quickly, Tom led them to the place where they could board the DOWN car and they scampered aboard. Well, the kids did, at least. Mimi had to squeeze all her fancy dress through the door. And Papa, who was tall, could not decide whether to go in

head first or back in. But soon, they were all tucked inside the small, little capsule.

Just as the door started to close, a hand held it open. "Mind if I join you?" a man said. "There's room for five passengers, you know."

Tom peeked in the door at Mimi and gave her an apologetic look. Mimi just smiled at him. "Of course," she told the man. "But please hurry."

The man climbed aboard. As he did, the rose in his tuxedo lapel was jostled off and fell into Christina's lap. The door closed and with a jerk, they started down.

Christina held her breath the whole way down. She felt like she was turning blue for the whole three minutes. The man watched Mimi the whole way down. Papa watched the man watch Mimi; it made him frown. Grant watched out the little windows.

Christina thought about the elevator at the hotel. Surely the power wouldn't go out? Surely they wouldn't stop? Surely they would get to the bottom and get out of this thing before the man said or did something bad?

Then Christina realized that she was just letting her imagination run away with her, as Mimi would say. This was just an ordinary man, probably going to the

same big deal event that they were. Wasn't he?

With a soft jolt, the car stopped and the door opened. Christina finally breathed. The man in the tux got out first, then held his hand to help Mimi, then Christina out of the car. Christina took his hand, but she would not look at him.

When they were finally back out in the fresh night air, the man seemed to have vanished. Mimi swished her skirt around to get it straight.

"Let's get going," Papa said.

Christina looked around for Sam but did not see him anywhere.

"It's gone!" Mimi suddenly yelped. She turned this way and that. "My purse is gone!"

"Well, do you really need it right now?" Papa asked. "We can look for it later. Maybe you just left it in the room?"

"No I didn't!" Mimi insisted. "I had it with me in the arch. And I have to have it—it has my speech in it, which I have to give in . . ." Another look at the watch: "In ten minutes!"

19. TIME FLIES WHEN YOU'RE NOT HAVING FUN

"You go get your seat," Papa said. "I will check the Lost and Found, then even go back to the hotel. I will bring you your speech—I promise!" He gave Mimi a quick kiss and ran across the grass.

Mimi hurried the kids along to the museum. It was crowded and everyone was moving slowly. People were in a festive mood. They stopped every few feet to greet someone or admire their outfit.

Mimi was in a panic. She finally finagled her way through the crowd, tugging Christina behind her. Christina held tightly to Grant's hand and tugged him along behind her.

Soon they were at their table. Mimi sat down and began to talk to Sam's Mom and Dad who were already seated. Christina heard her tell them the whole tale of the missing purse and speech.

Christina settled down by Sam.

"What's up?" he whispered.

"I'm not sure," Christina whispered back. "The man with the rose rode down the arch with us. It was so weird! And now, Mimi's purse and speech have disappeared. Papa's gone to hunt for it."

Before they could continue their conversation, the lights dimmed and a woman dressed in a black dress, glittering with sequins, appeared on the stage before them.

"LADIES AND GENTLEMEN!" she said. "Welcome to our Lewis and Clark celebration! We are so excited to have you here this evening. And we are really excited about our speaker, who will be . . ."

Before the woman could continue, another woman slipped up onto the stage and handed the first woman a note. The woman read it to herself, then nodded.

"Ladies and gentlemen," she continued. "We have a slight change. Our speech tonight will be given by Mr. Michael Fink. Please give him a hand!"

As everyone began to applaud, Mimi gasped. She could not understand what was happening! No one at their table could. However, no one else in the

audience knew what was going on, so they just clapped for the man who appeared on the stage in the spotlight. Mimi looked like she might cry.

"It's him!" Christina whispered to Sam.

And sure enough, the man on the stage wore a tuxedo with a fresh rose in the lapel.

"He must own a floral shop," Sam said.

There was nothing to do but sit there politely. The man smiled broadly. Christina thought he looked like he was really stuck on himself. Even though the cameras from the newspaper and television stations took pictures, the man stood there far too long without saying a word. He just grinned proudly.

Finally, the woman who had introduced him cleared her throat loudly ("Argh!") then louder ("Arrghh!") then so loud ("ARRGGHHHHHH!") that people at the front tables giggled.

The man pulled the microphone closer, and finally began to speak.

"AHEM—Long ago and far away people who had come to the New World clung to the edge of our continent," he began very dramatically.

Mimi gasped, "Ah!"

"But soon they grew brave, then braver," the man continued. *"They felt the urge to see what lay beyond their new home. What lay to the west. They packed their bags and left homes and loved ones behind."*

Mimi gasped louder, "AHHHH!"

Sam's Mom and Dad tried to quiet her down. "Are you okay?" they whispered. "Can we help you out to the lobby for some fresh air?"

But Christina had seen that look on her grandmother's face before. It was a look of defiance. Of determination. Of anger. A look like someone who could catch a bear with her bare hands—then eat it—hair and all!

Suddenly Christina realized why. She listened to the man closely now.

"And they headed west to seek their fame and fortune," he crooned.

Where had she heard those words before, Christina wondered. Recently. Very recently. Then she knew! It was this afternoon while she was falling asleep in the chair in the hotel room. As Mimi had been working on her speech at the computer, she had been reading out loud. Those were the words Mimi had written! How dare that man! What was going on?

Suddenly, Christina jumped up. "That's not your speech!" she screamed at the man. "You're a speech thief!"

Then Mimi jumped up. "STOP HIM!" she screamed. "HE STOLE MY SPEECH!"

Now the people at the round tables in the room looked about in confusion. The woman on the stage did not know what to do. The dining hall was buzzing with conversation about what in the world was going on. The man on the stage just grinned. It was clear he was planning to finish "his" speech.

Just then, Papa ran into the room. He ran right up to their table. He smiled broadly and waved a sheaf of white papers in one hand. "I've got it!" he shouted to Mimi. "I've got your speech. I found it!"

20 P IS FOR PLAGIARISM

When Papa saw the tears streaming down Mimi's face, he became very angry. Suddenly he realized what was happening. He gave the man on the stage an angry glare, then started up the stairs after him.

Several people in the audience screamed. Someone called for the "Cops!"

Mimi plopped back down in her chair.

Christina and Sam jumped up out of their chairs and ran toward the stage. Now Papa was on the stage. He grabbed the man by the sleeve of his tuxedo jacket. The man pulled away. Suddenly, the man ran toward the front of the stage. With a look of fear and panic, he closed his eyes and jumped.

When he fell overboard, he landed on his hands and knees. The breath had been knocked out of him.

Christina and Sam didn't help that at all—They sat on him! Suddenly, the spotlight swirled around and lighted up the scene for everyone to see: A downed man, a grinning boy, and a girl with a rose in her now very messy hair!

For awhile the hall was chaos. The police did show up. Papa came back down off the stage and explained. Mimi put in her two-cents-worth.

The policeman tried to piece the story together so it made some sense. "So you mean," he began. "That you (he pointed to Mimi) wrote a speech...and you (he pointed to Christina) got clues but couldn't figure them out...and you (he pointed to Papa) found the speech...but he (he pointed to the bad guy) was already giving the speech...and you (he pointed to Grant)..."

"Did nothing!" Grant promised, shoving his Boy Scout pledge fingers into the air. "I promise!"

For a moment it was quiet. Then the policeman said, "So this guy in the tuxedo is guilty of...guilty of...guilty of exactly what?"

"PLAGIARISM!" Sam cried suddenly. Then he

looked too embarrassed to speak further.

"That's what he did," Christina told the policeman. "He plagiarized my grandmother's speech and tried to make everyone think it was his own. It's stealing!"

When the policeman looked unsure, Christina, Sam, Mimi, and Papa, and Sam's mother and father all screamed in unison: "IT IS!"

And so the policeman arrested the man and hauled him away.

21 OLD MAN RIVER

Later that night, they all had put on their jeans and tee shirts and sneakers and were laying on the ground on a big quilt beneath the Gateway Arch.

"So what was that all about earlier tonight?" Sam's Dad asked. "I'm still confused. I feel like I came in the middle of a movie."

Mimi laughed. "I know the feeling!" she said. "But we learned more at the police station. That guy had been following us since New Orleans. He is a college student there, and flunking out, I think. His major course of study is journalism. Somehow he knew who I was. It seems he thought that he could steal words easier than he could write them. He thought that if he could make a speech at this major conference, he could get college credit and make a name for himself in the writing world—especially with

all the media that was there tonight."

"So he followed you all this way?" Sam's Mom asked.

"Yes!" Christina blurted. "I kept thinking I saw a man I recognized. He looked like that mime in Jackson Square. But when I saw him on the *Delta Queen* he talked to me—and mimes don't talk."

Papa frowned. "Of course, they do, Christina," he said. "They can talk as well as you and I can, only they just don't speak during their act."

"He stole Mimi's computer," Grant said. He had gone to the police station, too, and had a ball getting his fingerprints taken—his favorite souvenir, he said.

"But he was really just after the disk with her speech on it," Christina added.

"Only he didn't know she hadn't finished it," Grant added.

"But he must have when he printed it out," Mimi said.

"And that's why he followed us to the hotel and then up in the Gateway Arch where he stole Mimi's purse and finally got his hands on the final speech," Papa concluded.

Seeing St. Louis from the ground!

"And he kept following Christina, distracting her with silly clues, and trying to get information from her—like where we were staying in St. Louis," Mimi complained.

Everyone paused to think about the matter for a moment, then Grant spoke up. "So is he a river rogue?"

Papa laughed. "You bet he is! And a hooligan. And a . . ."

Christina began to roll on the grass in laughter.

"What's so funny?" Mimi said. She was going to get to give her speech tomorrow night, so she wasn't sad anymore.

"That dumb guy not only stole your speech, he even stole his pen name!" Christina said. "Michael Fink? Why that's just like Mike Fink, the riverman."

"Well," said Sam. "I guess he'll have a lot of time to do homework while he's in the hoosegow for the next two years."

"Whose gow?" Jake asked.

"Hoosegow," said Papa. "It's an old-timey word for jail, calaboose, clinker."

Again, they grew quiet, the kids trying to think of two looooong years of non-stop homework.

"Old," said Grant. "He's gonna be an old man when he gets outta there." He gave Papa a funny look, and Papa gave him a wink.

"Oh, nooooo," Christina groaned.

"What's wrong?" Sam asked.

"Just watch!" said Christina.

And sure enough, Grant and Papa grabbed one another and began to sing—at the tip top of their lungs, so loudly everyone around them began to stare—

"OLD MAN RIVER,
THAT OLD MAN RIVER,
HE DON'T SAY NOTHIN,
HE JUST KEEPS ROLLIN,
HE JUST KEEPS ROLLIN
ALOOOOOOOONG!"

Then fortunately, before they could start another verse, the fireworks show began and drowned them out. The shiny steel arch glittered as it reflected the pinks and blues and greens of the sparkling firecrackers.

Christina sat back against Mimi's lap and looked up at the Gateway Arch. It looks like an upside-

down smile, she thought to herself. Then she smiled at her family, always involved in mystery, always sticking together, and always having fun!

The End

ABOUT THE AUTHOR

Carole Marsh is an author and publisher who has written many works of fiction and non-fiction for young readers. She travels throughout the United States and around the world to research her books. In 1979 Carole Marsh was named Communicator of the Year for her corporate communications work with major national and international corporations.

Marsh is the founder and CEO of Gallopade International, established in 1979. Today, Gallopade International is widely recognized as a leading source of educational materials for every state and many countries. Marsh and Gallopade were recipients of the 2004 Teachers' Choice Award. Marsh has written more than 16 Carole Marsh Mysteries™. Years ago, her children, Michele and Michael, were the original characters in her mystery books. Today, they continue the Carole Marsh Books tradition by working at Gallopade. By adding grandchildren Grant and Christina as new mystery characters, she has continued the tradition for a third generation.

Ms. Marsh welcomes correspondence from her readers. You can e-mail her at carole@gallopade.com, visit the carolemarshmysteries.com website, or write to her in care of Gallopade International, P.O. Box 2779, Peachtree City, Georgia, 30269 USA.

GLOSSARY

barge: a long, flat boat that has no power, but is just used to load goods on; it is pushed along by a tugboat

bateau: (pronounced bah toe); French name for a small boat

broadhorn: a type of river boat

cordelle: to tow a boat with a rope

dam: a stone or earthen wall to hold back a river

keelboat, flatboat: type of simple boats that once went up and down the Mississippi River

levees: dams or dikes made of dirt, stone, or metal to hold back floodwaters

locks: a set of walls to hold back or let in water, so a boat could move up or down the river where a falls once was

pirogue: a small boat made from a hollow tree trunk

shoals: sandy areas in a river

snags and sawyers: logs and other debris in the water that can damage a boat

SCAVENGER HUNT!

Find out one fact about each of these Mississippi River related things! *Teachers: you have permission to reproduce this form for your students.*

__1.   river rogues

__2.   locks and dams

__3.   The Gateway Arch

__4.   New Orleans, Louisiana

__5.   earthquakes

__6.   list all the states that border the Mississippi River!

__7.   The 1904 World's Fair in St. Louis

__8.   Mark Twain

__9.   Tom Sawyer

__10. The *Delta Queen*

WRITE YOUR OWN MYSTERY!

Make up a dramatic title!

You can pick four real kid characters!

Select a real place for the story's setting!

Try writing your first draft!

Edit your first draft!

Read your final draft aloud!

You can add art, photos or illustrations!

Share your book with others and send me a copy!

Six Secret Writing Tips from Carole Marsh!

Non-fiction is factual!

1. Make up good titles – wild and crazy is good!

2. Use strong verbs – action verbs with pizzazz!

3. Edit your work to make it better!

4. Use your own special "voice" to make your work unique!

5. Use a thesaurus and dictionary to find the words that mean what you want to say!

6. Don't worry about rules – use your imagination and have fun!

Fiction is made up!

WOULD YOU ~~MYSTERIES~~ LIKE TO BE A CHARACTER IN A CAROLE MARSH MYSTERY?

If you would like to star in a Carole Marsh Mystery, fill out the form below and write a 25-word paragraph about why you think you would make a good character! Once you're done, ask your mom or dad to send this page to:

Carole Marsh Mysteries Fan Club
Gallopade International
P.O. Box 2779
Peachtree City, GA 30269

My name is: _____

I am a: ____boy ____girl   Age: _____

I live at: _____

City: _____

State:_____ Zip code: _____

My e-mail address:_____

My phone number is:_____

_____

_____

_____

_____

_____

_____

_____

_____

Enjoy this exciting excerpt from

THE MYSTERY AT THE KENTUCKY DERBY

1 THOROUGHBREDS IN THE MIST

A thick, swirling fog hung low over the ground in the cool air of the pre-dawn darkness. The rich moisture had settled on every surface. Billions of tiny droplets reflected what little light penetrated the fog. The fence rail where Christina and Grant stood stretched away to their left. Eerily glistening in the bluish light from the Churchill Downs grandstand, the railing faded away into the fog.

Christina and Grant peered through the mist at the wide expanse of dirt between the outside and inside rail. Across the track, near the big white column that marked the finish line, stood three men. Their dark silhouettes were punctuated by the blue-green glow of a digital stopwatch.

The sound of a lone horse at full gallop came from far in the distance, the hoofbeats muted by the mist.

"He's entering the third turn," Sara said quietly.

Christina, nine years old, turned away from the track to look at Sara, the ten-year-old daughter of Mimi's friend. Mimi, Christina's grandmother, had brought her and her brother Grant to Louisville, Kentucky for the 130th running of the Kentucky Derby.

"How do you know?" Christina asked. She rubbed her arms to rid them of the creepy goosebumps.

"The hoofbeats stopped moving away from us," Sara explained.

"Wow! You've got good hearing!" Grant, Christina's seven-year-old brother, whispered excitedly.

"It's creepy sometimes," said Tanner, Sara's twelve-year-old cousin. "You can't sneak up on her."

"Shh!" Sara hissed. "Quarter-mile," she said, and stood up to grip the wet rail.

Tanner moved up beside her, and the four of them focused on the fogged-up Home Stretch. Some called this short 1/4-mile-long patch of dirt Heartbreak Lane, because it was where the Kentucky Derby was really won or lost.

The hoofbeats grew louder as the horse raced up the home stretch. The gallop became faster as the invisible horse put forth a final surge of speed.

Then, as if caught in slow-motion mid-stride and seeming to float on the fog, the horse and jockey burst into sight. Curls of fog swirled in the horse's wake like the tentacles of a ghostly octopus. Dirt flew up from the horse's hoof steps in shadowy globs.

The horse passed the finish line and flew by the four kids in a streak of dark hair and yellow silk. Christina watched the horse and jockey disappear into the fogbank as the gallop began to slow down.

Grant giggled excitedly. "Oh, man!" he exclaimed. "That was fast!"

"Not fast enough," Tanner said.

"What do you mean?" Christina asked.

"What's his time?" Sara asked.

Tanner held up his stopwatch for them to see. Black numbers floated in the blue-green glow: 2:09.13.

"Two minutes, nine point one-three seconds," Sara moaned. "That *is* slow."

"If that's slow," Grant began, "then what's *fast*?"

"The closer to two minutes, the better," Sara explained. "That—" she pointed at the stopwatch— "is seven seconds off the average time to win the Derby."

Christina peered down the track past Tanner and Sara as the racehorse cantered back toward the finish line and the three men. It was a dreamy, fairy tale-like sight. The horse's dark shape glided through the mist at a trot's pace, with the jockey sitting tall on his back. The yellow silk of his shirt and the horse's saddlecloth shimmered in the light from the grandstand.

After a minute, the jockey turned the Thoroughbred back down the track, and they trotted off. Two of the three men disappeared into the fog over the infield, but one had hopped over the inside rail and was approaching them.

"Is that your Dad?" Christina asked Sara.

"It is," Sara replied. "And I'll bet he's disappointed. Skit usually runs fast in the morning."

"Hiyo, kids," Sara's Dad called. "Whatcha think? Have we got a winner, or what?"

"I'll bet you do," Grant said happily. "That horse is fast!"

"Looks good to me," Christina chimed in.

"Hmmm," Tanner hummed skeptically.

"He was slow this morning, Dad," Sara said sadly.

"That's okay," Dad said. "We were trying something a little different in the running."

"I guess it didn't work," Sara said.

"Not the way we expected," Dad replied. They fell silent as the sound of a starting bell pierced through the foggy darkness. The hoofbeats of another horse making an early morning run quickly blurred from a trot to a canter to a gallop. Christina and Grant scooted away from the rail so Sara's Dad could jump over.

The horse streaked by and disappeared into the fog, its hoofbeats quickly fading.

An electronic tone chirped from the wireless phone on Sara's Dad's waist.

"*Charles...*" a hurried voice said.

Charles lifted the phone to his mouth. "What is it, Earl?"

"*We need you in the stable,*" Earl said anxiously. "*Lickety-Split is pitching a fit. He's been going on since before we got back— screaming and kicking up a storm. Something's got him spooked!*"

THE CAROLE MARSH MYSTERIES SERIES

VISIT THE CAROLE MARSH MYSTERIES WEBSITE

www.carolemarshmysteries.com

- *Check out what's coming up next! Are we coming to your area with our next book release? Maybe you can have your book signed by the author!*

- *Join the Carole Marsh Mysteries Fan Club!*

- *Apply for the chance to be a character in an upcoming Carole Marsh Mystery!*

- *Learn how to write your own mystery!*